THINGS

Peter Cherches

BAMBOO DART PRESS

LOS ANGELES † NEW YORK † LONDON † MELBOURNE

Things by Peter Cherches

ISBN: 978-1-947240-74-2   Paperback

ISBN: 978-1-947240-75-9   eBook

First Printing 2023

Cover art by Dennis Callaci

Layout and design by Mark Givens

Author photo by Elder Zamora

For information:

Bamboo Dart Press

chapbooks@bamboodartpress.com

Bamboo Dart Press 035

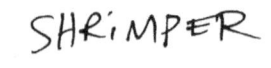

www.pelekinesis.com   www.bamboodartpress.com   www.shrimperrecords.com

*For all the editors who have offered square holes to my
square pegs.*

Grateful acknowledgment is made to the following journals, anthologies, and websites in which many of these pieces first appeared:

101 Words, Danse Macabre, Five Plus Five, Flash Boulevard, Gargoyle, Love in the Time of COVID, Mono, MoonPark Review, Mothers of Mud, MungBeing, Otoliths, Rune Bear, Six Sentences, South Florida Poetry Journal, Star 82, Sulfur: Surrealist Jungle, Synchronized Chaos.

CONTENTS

CORNERED

I find myself in a corner. Of a page or a room, I can't tell. It's white, the page or the room. That's little help. Rooms are often white, and pages more often. Are those words I see, or furniture? Rooms are often white, the furniture says.

I find myself in a room of words, a furnished page. A page with a view, or a room with a point of view. I'd like to know how it would feel to dip my toe into this sentence.

No different, really, than any other dip of the toe. I could discourse for hours on toe dipping, both literal and figurative, but hours of discourse on toe dipping would be rather ironic, don't you think?

I'm trying to work my way out of the corner. It's work. I don't know how I found myself in the corner in the first place. I wasn't backed into it, not that I can remember.

Could it be a third thing? What would that be if not a page and not a room? Could a third thing be both not a page and not a room and both a page and a room?

I find myself in a corner. Of a third thing. Not a page. Not a room. Perhaps a pageroom. Or a roompage.

Would it make any difference?

I find myself in a corner of a roompage. I survey the roompage, my roompage, from the corner, my corner.

And I am pleased.

ANOTHER THING

She told me I had another thing coming to me, so I waited for the thing. It's not that I really needed another thing, I had plenty of things as it was, some might say too many things, but still, if I had another thing coming to me I wanted to see what it was, and then I could decide if it was just one of those things I'd move to the back of my mind and forget about or if it was something I should concern myself with. So I waited.

Nothing came to me that really fit the bill of another thing; oh sure there were little things here and there, but certainly nothing that would qualify as another thing. I was starting to get pissed off. Where was that other thing already? Screw this, I told myself, I'm just going to come right out and ask her.

So I asked her.

"What was that other thing?" I asked her.

"What other thing?"

"You know, the other thing you told me I had coming to me."

"When was that?"

"You know, yesterday, when we were discussing this and that!"

"Oh that!" she said. "I was probably just pissed off!"

Pissed off? She was pissed off? She tells me I have another

thing coming to me and she's pissed off? What does she have to be pissed off about? I'm the one who should be pissed off!

"What were you pissed off about?"

"Oh, you know," she said. "This and that."

THIS AND THAT

She was startled and alarmed. He was surprised and shocked. She was incredulous and envious. He was apologetic and overweight. She was wild and wooly. He was suave and deferential. She was perky and well-caffeinated. He was ecstatic and erratic. She was sweet and sour. He was pork and beans. She was wan and wanton. He was a little of this, a little of that. They were made for each other.

HOW TO READ THIS STORY

Read it with a hat on, just as you'd wear a fedora for *The Long Goodbye*, a beret for Sartre's *Nausea*, or a woman's hat, what woman's hat, for what book or story? The Trilby hat does not appear in the novel *Trilby*. Choose a hat, a hat you're comfortable in or a hat you'd feel ridiculous wearing. It all boils down to this: What kind of reader are you?

Read it not as a set of instructions, but rather follow the clues to wherever they may lead you.

First read the words, then turn away and imagine yourself reading the words.

Now try to divine the story's story. If you succeed, you've done my job.

Congratulations! You may take the hat off now.

Return Authorization

To Whom It May Concern,

I'm writing in reference to the item I purchased on June 17, order number HJ74002. I received the item yesterday, and am pleased to report that it was neatly and securely packaged, arrived within the stated delivery window, and was intact and unblemished. Unfortunately, it was not the item I ordered. In fact, it bore no resemblance, in form or function, to the thing I ordered, and which, I might add, I was so looking forward to, having scoured the internet for years with no luck until I happened upon your website, with which I was previously unfamiliar. But the item I received was, in fact, of an entirely different category, so different, indeed, that it boggles the mind that two items so wildly unrelated could even be sold by the same retailer, the moniker "superstore" notwithstanding. I mean, imagine ordering a package of coconut-chocolate sandwich cookies and receiving an atomic bomb instead. Of course, I'm just using those two items as an example. I did not order coconut-chocolate sandwich cookies, and I did not receive an atomic bomb, I just used those two items to forcefully and, admittedly, with poetic license convey my shock and surprise upon receiving an item so utterly different from the one I ordered, but I could have mentioned any number of things, a potato peeler and an emu, for instance. In any case, I would like to return the item received in error for a full refund; please send me a return authorization along with instructions on how to package the item safely and securely so as not to blow my home, if not my city, or even the entire nation—possibly, in a worst-case scenario, the whole wide world—to kingdom come.

Sincerely,

HOMAGE TO KAWABATA

I had it in the palm of my hand, the left one. It was a small book, written in the lines. It wasn't a fortune, not even a small one, it was for the mass market. I started reading. "Once upon a time there was a place," it began. The whole story took place in the lines. In the palm of my hand. It was a small book, but a big story. A blockbuster. I tried it out. It worked like a charm. I busted a block of concrete, barehanded, with my left palm. It turned out there was a book embedded in the concrete block, now loose. I picked it up and looked at the cover. It was called *Palm-of-the-Hand Stories*, the author Yasunari Kawabata.

FLAVORS

The thin, flat, square thing has a slightly metallic, alkaline taste.

The small sphere, about the size of a marble, though not a fruit, is tart, citrus tart.

The irregular white pebble with the violet veins is the salt of the sea crashing against a craggy shoreline.

The concave vessel, though dry and empty, evokes a strong olfactory and gustatory sensation of blood—iron-rich, vibrant blood.

The hairy patch, vaguely pubic, but inconclusive, has a flavor profile reminiscent of the famous white truffles of Alba, musky and aromatic. But, naturally, it is far less dear.

No Name

She came and she went. She came and she went. She came and she went and she didn't have a name.

She came. She came. She came without a name. She went and she came. She went and she came. She went and she came and she didn't have a name.

She had a face. She had a voice. She had a face she had a voice but she didn't have a name. She went and she came and she didn't have a name.

She came. She came. She came without a name. She came and she came and she came. And she went. She went. She went without a name.

She came. She came. With a voice and a face she came. She came and she came and she didn't have a name.

She didn't have a name. She came. With a voice she came. With a face she came. And she went she went she went without a name.

She went without a name she came. She came without a name. She came and she came and she came. And she went. She went. With a voice and a face and a face and a voice and she went and she came no name, no name.

MOOD INDIGO

Something thinking, something sleeping, softly thinking, something blue. Some something finds loving, some slumber comes slowly, some lover sings something, keeps singing slowly. Slow singing keeps loving gently, loves slowly, sings something blue, comes gently. Some lover sings, some lover sleeps, sleeps slowly, sleeps gently, some thinking, some blue thing.

SCREAM!

It is better to scream than to be screamed at,
So go ahead and scream!

Scream for every kernel on every ear of corn in every cornfield
in Iowa.
Scream for a time when gold doubloons are no longer
necessary for the short-term rental of a phosphorescent
tree house in a virgin wood.
Scream for all the catatonic pilgrims on the road to nowhere.

Scream for Christopher Marlowe.
Scream for Philip Marlowe.
Scream for the amoebae, the protozoa, the paramecia.
Scream for all the juke joints in all the emergency rooms of all
the papier-mâché palaces.
Scream for the glen plaid-clad elocutionists who come
knocking at your door.
Scream for all the dead pet turtles flushed down the toilets of
New York City by indifferent children of the sixties.
Scream for the plumbers.
Scream for the right to whimper.
Scream for brushes, and bobby pins, and carburetors, and
noodles.
Scream for the sad, abandoned clam diggers.
Scream for the wall-eyed pike, because if you don't, who will?
Scream for an end to calcified beginnings.
And scream for those who'd rather you didn't.

Just get out there,
Open your mouth as wide as you dare,
And scream!

STRANDGALLIER

I wanted to buy a new strandgallier, as my old and trusty one was on its last legs. The shop my father had bought it from just before I was born, Lindemann's, was long gone, and I couldn't think of anywhere nearby that might carry them, so I decided to look online. No luck on Amazon, so I tried Ebay. Surely someone must be selling a strandgallier on Ebay. Even a used one in good to excellent condition would do, but there were none to be found on Ebay, used or new. Then I thought maybe Google Shopping might yield results from some further-flung corners of the internet. I typed "strandgallier" in the search box but got no exact match, which is not to say I got no results. The first match was a Strandberg Boden Masvidalien NX 6 Cosmo, an electric guitar. Kind of amusing to see an electric guitar when what you're looking for is a strandgallier. But an even bigger stretch was the Safavieh BCH1000D Bandelier Bench. Did the search algorithm think my typing was slurred? What good is a search engine that conflates strandgallier with bandelier? And I certainly wasn't looking for a Stranda Descender Split 22/23 Splitboard. I haven't the slightest idea what a splitboard is. I just wanted a simple, garden-variety strandgallier.

Could they be discontinued? It happens all too often. A great product that fits your need to a T (or is it tee or tea?) just goes the way of the dodo. Nobody steps in to make a replacement, perhaps because it's too much of a niche product.

I just might need to find a repair shop, I surmised. There are people who can repair anything, right?

So I searched for "strandgallier repair," but got no satisfaction. There was a tweet from a cake baker praising the customer service at the Aldi UK in Banbury, where "After delayed mother & baby delivery a poor henpecked CSA helped me find the products I wanted!" Surely, "henpecked" is not the word she was looking for, or was the poor CSA complaining about the trouble and strife while servicing the woman? Maybe "harried" is what she meant to say. And fat lot of good a GORE-TEX repair shop would do me either.

This was all taking too much time, so I decided to give up, for the time being. My strandgallier may be on its last legs, but it still does the job, albeit with lots of crunching and wheezing sounds. So I guess I'll just live with the noise until it breaks down completely, and then I'll worry about repairs. Who knows, it's been going for almost 67 years, it may even outlive me, in which case my nephew Danny, to whom I've bequeathed it in my will, will have to deal with it.

LIMITED EDITION

Only five were ever produced, a very limited edition, handcrafted by artisans who were fed the tradition as mother's milk. Two are in private collections, two in craft or folk art museums, and one is unaccounted for—it was last seen in Poland in 1939.

To Shelly Kaminsky, who has the fifth one hanging on her living room wall, it's just a tchotchke she retrieved from the house when her mother died. She knows nothing of its provenance, its rarity, its quality, but she remembers it from when she was a kid.

Just a little reminder of Mom, who never wanted to talk about Poland.

THE LONELINESS VENDOR

The loneliness vendor is running a sale. 'Half off my loneliness,' his sign says. Still no takers. Who wants to acquire the state of a sad, lonely man?

Then a very famous person, a superstar, happens upon the loneliness vendor in his attempt to evade a throng of persistent paparazzi.

The star buys the man's loneliness, hoping this will provide cover, the asking price a trifle to a man of means such as he.

"Where did he go?" the paparazzi ask the once-famous man.

"Over there," he tells them, pointing toward the once-lonely man, now thronged by fawning admirers, suffocating, miserable.

A Dry One

It was pouring rain, and the gift was getting drenched. The stupid man hadn't brought an umbrella, even though there was heavy rain in the forecast, and anyone could have seen the dark, ominous clouds just by looking out the window.

It was an anniversary gift for Delilah, his wife. They had been married 25 years, a milestone, though he couldn't remember which metal. They'd had their ups and downs, sure, but what couple doesn't? Michael had his share of affairs over the years, a whole string of them, but they were mere diversions. Delilah, on the other hand, was only unfaithful with one other man, Michael's cousin William; they had met at Michael and Delilah's wedding and first slept with each other the following weekend, when she had snuck out under subterfuge. The affair was still going on, all these years later, and Michael still hadn't a clue.

When Michael presented her with the anniversary gift, Delilah was appalled by the soaking piece of crap. What kind of gift was that for a 25th anniversary? Or any anniversary, for that matter.

So she walked out on Michael and moved in with William, who had a dry one.

PLACEMENT

"I think it would look better over there," she said, pointing over there.

He picked it up and moved it over there. "There," he said, "what do you think?"

"I don't know," she said. "Something's not quite right. Maybe if you shift it a little to the left?"

Without a word he shifted it to the left.

"No," she said, "that's not it either. I don't know what it is."

"Maybe if you gave it a few days," he suggested. "Maybe you just need to get used to it."

She gave it a few days.

"Nope," she said, "still not doing it for me."

"Maybe a little to the right?" he suggested.

"Give it a try."

He moved it to the right. It was now exactly where he had first placed it when he brought it over there, before he moved it a little to the left.

"Yes," she said, "I think that's it. Perfect!"

HAIKU

there are just some things
you don't say in a haiku
like this for instance

DIALOGUE

"It is what it is."
"Whatever."
"It is what it is."
"Whatever."
"It is what it is."
"Whatever."
"It is what it is."
"Whatever."
"It is what it is."
"Whatever."
"It is what it is."
"Whatever."
"It is what it is."
"Whatever."
"It is what it is."
"Whatever."
"It is what it is."
"Whatever."
"It is what it is."
"Whatever."
"It is what it is."

"Whatever."

"It is what it is."

"Whatever."

"It is what it is."

"Whatever."

"It is what it is."

"Whatever."

"It is what it is."

"Whatever."

"It is what it is."

"Whatever."

THE BROTH

"This broth is spoiled," said the king's food taster. "Send in the cook!"

"Cooks plural," said the royal secretary.

"Plural?" said the food taster. "How many cooks are there?"

"Oh, more than enough, I assure you," said the secretary. "More than enough."

THE METAMORPHOSIS

As Ludlow St. John awoke one morning from uneasy dreams he found himself transformed in his bed into a thing. A mere thing. No longer Ludlow St. John, no longer a man, not a person, just a thing—and not even a specific thing, nothing more than a generic thing. This, thought the thing formerly Ludlow St. John, is surely the uneasiest dream of all; I've lost my self, my humanity, to mere objecthood, thought no-longer-Ludlow. And then, no longer thoughts, no memory, no past, just thinghood unto eternity.

When the workmen came to clean out the apartment of the unknown disappeared tenant—nobody, not even the landlord, could remember his name—one of the men came upon something atop the bed. He turned it over and saw, embossed on the bottom, "Ludlow St. John," which meant nothing to him. So he threw it out the window, just barely missing an old woman passing by.

Russian Novel

Semyon Semyonovich had misplaced his thing. He discovered this fact one cold November St. Petersburg morning in the year of 1867. "My thing! My thing is gone!" he shouted upon awakening, surveying his room, and discovering that his thing was gone. Semyon Semyonovich's manservant, Grisha, ran into his master's bedroom upon hearing the racket.

"Is something wrong, sir?" Grisha asked.

"It's my thing, man, my thing!"

"What is the problem, sir?"

"My thing, it's my thing, it's gone!"

"Your thing is gone?"

"What did I just say?"

"You said, 'My thing, it's my thing, it's gone!'"

"Yes," said Semyon Semyonovich, "that's exactly what I said. So what kind of nincompoop asks someone who says, 'My thing, it's my thing, it's gone!' if his thing is gone?"

"I am so sorry," Grisha said, fearful and tearful, as he dropped to his knees and licked his master's boots.

"And another thing, you idiot," Semyon Semyonovich said. "Wait till I put my damn boots on before you lick them!"

ONE-SENTENCE STORIES

Like a Leap Year

She carried on as if life were a day longer, like a leap year.

Unfinished Symphony

"I never did get around to starting that unfinished symphony of mine," the composer lamented on his deathbed.

Orphans

When our father died, we were ready to go to the orphanage, then we remembered, we lived with our mother, who was still alive.

A Gershwin Tune

"They can't take that away from me," I sang, as they took it away from me.

Phantom Pain

I experienced a phantom pain where my despair used to be.

Life on Earth

Life on earth having become untenable, I packed my bags and moved into my daydreams.

After the Ball

After the ball was over, the chain returned to its master.

The Last Bus

He had no idea the world was going to end in minutes, he was just relieved he had caught the last bus of the night.

ON THE DEATH OF THE POET'S MOTHER

from Selected Poems of Jean Trucage, *translated by Peter Cherches*

Mother, never again will I smell the smell of the bread you
    baked.
Never again will your back trouble you,
Never again will I serve you café au lait in bed because your
    back troubles you.

Never again will you call Uncle Maurice a dumbell,
Never again will you call Cousin Danielle a tramp,
Never again will you call LeDuc the baker a cheapskate,
Never again will you call Doctor Barzin a quack.

Mother, never again will you call me "my hope."
Never again will anybody call me "my hope."

A COUPLE

from Selected Poems of Jean Trucage, *translated by Peter Cherches*

and they lived
and they died
and no one ever knew
except the birds
and their dog
Maurice

An Experiment

I decided to try an experiment. I put a table in the center of the empty room. I took a wood block, a cube, with a different color on each side: red, green, blue, orange, yellow, and purple. I placed the cube on the table, left the room, and closed the door. Five minutes later I went back into the room and there was a ball on the table in place of the cube, a rubber ball, about the same volume as the wooden cube, a red rubber ball. I knew there was no hanky-panky going on. Nobody was in the room when I entered, and nobody had access after I had left. I left the room again and closed the door.

I returned five minutes later to discover that the ball was now green. Interesting, I thought. Repeat.

Next time I went into the room the ball was blue. The same blue as one of the sides of the cube, just as the previous colors had exactly matched those on the cube. It was a deep blue, the kind Mondrian used in his grid paintings, as was, come to think of it, the red. Something's definitely happening here, I thought.

Next iteration. When I returned to the room 20 minutes into the experiment the ball was orange, orange like the fruit, and it was pretty much the same size as a real orange. I could almost taste it. Nobody could deny I was making progress by this point. My heart started beating just a bit faster, but I tried to contain my excitement, because it ain't over till it's over. Another five minutes, same drill, and the ball was yellow, yellow like the sun. I hadn't noticed the "sun-ness" of the yellow when it was a side of the cube, but as a ball the sun came shining through. Yet the show must go on. I left the room again, for another five minutes. When I returned the ball was purple.

We were so close that I allowed myself a frisson of excitement. I left the room again, for the longest five minutes I've ever passed, and now my heart was pounding like Gene Krupa's drum solo on "Sing, Sing, Sing." I returned to the room and there it was—a purple cube, purple on all sides.

Success!

Not Quite Stories

1. My name is Sampson. Chester Sampson. People call me Sampson.

    "But how did you know about me and Danvers?" the conniving little blond called back to me, as they were taking her away.

    "It wasn't difficult, sweetheart," I told her. "Considering."

2. Daisy hadn't given him a second thought, yet there he was, on her doorstep, carrying a potted plant.

    "Remember me?" he asked.

3. "Things was hard back then," the old man told the visiting nurse.

    The nurse, who hadn't asked a question, didn't bother to wonder when "back then" was.

4. The brothers hadn't seen each other for over 20 years. Identical twins, they'd had a falling out, and they lived far from each other, on opposite coasts. This particular day, Tom had gone to shop for khakis at the Banana Republic in the mall near his home. When he entered the store, all eyes turned to him. He wondered why.

    Tim came out of the dressing room to look at himself in the full-length mirror, in his new khakis. As he looked into the mirror, Tim noticed Tom behind him, in the distance.

    Tim wondered how the reunion would go, but to his

relief, still staring into the mirror, he saw Tom turn around and leave the store.

5. My son-in-law found me in the kitchen, after my husband was gone. I asked him if he wanted a cup of coffee. He sat.

We sat together at the table, drinking coffee. Not another word passed between us.

6. "It was after the war," she told him.

"So, all of a sudden everything changed?"

"No," she replied, "not all and not so sudden."

7. After weeks of indecision, Cora finally decided to call that number. She pulled the piece of paper out of her purse and made the call. When it connected at the other end, she was surprised to be greeted by one of those pre-recorded menus. The choices were very confusing. She relied upon her instincts to tell her which path to choose. Unfortunately, it was the wrong one.

8. "Mr. Thorndike will see you now," the secretary told the man sitting on the blue-upholstered bentwood chair in the anteroom. The man's palms had been sweating, and he'd been rubbing them along his slacks above the knees.

The man got up and knocked on Thorndike's door.

"Come in," Thorndike yelled, in a neutral tone of voice.

The man went in.

He never came out.

9. He was driving. On the freeway. He looked up at the

sign, above and ahead. Belford 20 miles, Grainger next exit. He got off at the next exit.

She'd just have to wait.

10.

NONVIOLENCE

There was a fly on his nose, sitting on the tip of his nose.

"There's a fly on your nose," she told him.

"Yes, when I cross my eyes and look down I can see it."

"Doesn't it bother you?"

"Not in the least," he said.

And the fly flew away.

BETTER THAN THAT

"Is it edible?" she asked.

"I don't know," he said. "How do we find out?"

"Feed it to some animal, like a mouse, or a squirrel, or a raccoon, I suppose."

"That's so cruel," he said, "to risk the life of an animal, even a small one, a mammal no less, just to see if something's edible, just so we humans can enjoy it once we know it's safe?"

"Why not? I assume that's how people have always figured out whether things are edible, either by experimenting on themselves and living or dying or getting sick, or by seeing how an animal reacts."

"But we're better than people who would experiment on animals, aren't we?"

"You're right," she said. "You try it."

CLOUD-BIRD

Sometime in the distance, a cloud fell from the sky into a lake of feathers, pinfeathers, hardly suitable for a feather boa, so left alone by the boa poachers, who had bigger fish to fry. Upon meeting the feather lake, the cloud laid an egg. The cloud chick, featherless, could not distinguish itself from the body of feathers in which it hatched. The cloud had disavowed it, so the chick was left to its own devices, to fend for itself. The cloud reverted to water and soaked the feathers. The chick floated, treading wet feathers. Looking skyward, the chick could make out the fuzzy outline of a cloud. It dreamed of flight, believing the cloud above to be its mother. Gulls would stop by with small fish for the chick to feed upon, having resolved, at an emergency meeting of the flock, to care for it. The chick thrived. Emulating its guardian angels, the gulls, it taught itself to fly, this cloud-bird. It flew, far and high, to the cloud above, but the cloud turned a blind eye. So the bird became its own cloud.

THE NIGHT SKY

A man was looking through a book at the night sky. The clock struck an innocent bystander. "What hath God wrought?" an old woman shouted, quoting Samuel F.B. Morse. A funeral brass band passed, "St. James Infirmary." But there was no funeral this time, just a dry run.

"What do you say Mabel, just one little kiss?"

Mabel slapped Wallace's face. "We'll have none of your malarkey, Wally," she said, and then she kissed him right where she slapped him.

"Aw Mabel, I don't deserve you," Wallace said.

"That's the first sensible thing I've heard from your kisser in a dog's age," Mabel replied.

The trumpeter from the funeral band broke into a hora—or was it a freilach? The other musicians joined in. Wallace to Mabel: Shall we dance? But it was the wrong dance they danced, a tarantella. The cop on the beat noticed but decided not to get involved.

The book was a big disappointment, the man thought, but on a clear night like this the sky is a thing to behold.

How to Write an Effective Composition

Narrow down your subject
Then narrow it down some more
Narrow it down until there's nothing left
Now you're ready to begin

Then narrow it down some more
Until writing becomes impossible
Now you're ready to begin
And there's nothing left to say

Until writing becomes impossible
Writing effectively remains a necessity
And there's nothing left to say
But to say nothing

Writing effectively remains a necessity
And nothing is a solution
But to say nothing
Is something, after all

And nothing is a solution
Only in terms of the composition
Is something, after all
Developing here?

Only in terms of the composition
Is there a theme
Developing here?
Is an essay taking shape?

Is there a theme?
Narrow down your subject
Is an essay taking shape?
Narrow it down until there's nothing left

SACCO'S SPEECH

I am not an orator.
It is not very familiar with me the English language.
I never know, never heard, even read in history anything so
    cruel as this court.
After seven years prosecuting they still consider us guilty.

It is not very familiar with me the English language.
I know the sentence will be between two class, the oppressed
    class and the rich class.
After seven years prosecuting they still consider us guilty.
There will always be collision between one and the other.

I know the sentence will be between two class, the oppressed
    class and the rich class.
We fraternize the people with the books, with the literature.
There will always be collision between one and the other.
You persecute the people, tyrannize over them, and kill them.

We fraternize the people with the books, with the literature.
We try the education of people always.
You persecute the people, tyrannize over them, and kill them.
You try to put a path between us and some other nationality
    that hates each other.

We try the education of people always.
That is why I am here today on this bench, for having been the
    oppressed class.

You try to put a path between us and some other nationality
that hates each other.
Well, you are the oppressor.

That is why I am here today on this bench, for having been
the oppressed class.
I would like to tell you my life, but what is the use?
Well, you are the oppressor.
I am never be guilty, never—not yesterday nor today nor
forever.

I would like to tell you my life, but what is the use?
I never know, never heard, even read in history anything so
cruel as this court.
I am never be guilty, never—not yesterday nor today nor
forever.
I am not an orator.

UNWRITTEN POEM

I can take any blank page and call it
An unwritten poem.
That part is easy enough.
The real challenge is to write it.

An unwritten poem:
Naming it is nothing.
The real challenge is to write it
And yet write nothing.

Naming it is nothing.
But I would like to make this poem
And yet write nothing.
I want to make nothing tangible.

But I would like to make this poem
Something as real as warm flesh.
I want to make nothing tangible,
Something to hold when I'm alone.

Something as real as warm flesh.
I'd like to make nothing something and call it you,
Something to hold when I'm alone.
I want a poem more real than you.

I'd like to make nothing something and call it you.
Since I can't have you,
I want a poem more real than you—
My conception of you.

Since I can't have you,
I can take any blank page and call it
"My Conception of You."
That part is easy enough.

MOTHERS

I remember the beautiful mother who reminded me of Doris Day; the family moved away when I was six or seven. Her name was Rita.

I remember the mother who looked kind of like Shari Lewis—the puppeteer and kids' show host whose alter ego was Lamb Chop—and kind of like Gloria Okon—the weather lady on channel 11 who was also the spokesperson for Arnold bread. Curly strawberry blond hair. Cute and comforting. Not a bombshell like Rita, whose beauty was sometimes commented upon, with a mix of admiration and envy, by the other mothers in the neighborhood.

I remember the mother who looked like Shirley Booth in *Hazel*. She usually wore polyester stretch pants.

And I remember the mother of my best friend. She was one of my own mother's canasta buddies. At the time she didn't remind me of any movie actress or TV personality, but in retrospect I have an image of Anne Bancroft in *The Graduate*—perhaps because she once answered the door wrapped in nothing but a towel, straight out of the shower.

Bringing It Up

"I haven't thought about that in years," he told her when she brought it up.

"Oh really?" she said. "I've never stopped thinking about it."

UNBLOCKED

A writer, plagued by writer's block, trained himself to shit stories. It was a long and laborious process, as his guts had to form the turds into tiny letters, like the noodles in alphabet soup. But the writer was now incredibly productive. He'd produce a new story every day. Unfortunately, none of them were any good.

SECTS

Once nothing more than a piece of junk, it's now a venerated object. It is a venerated piece of junk, a sign of humility
for its worshippers. It is a humble piece of shit, venerated for
its shittiness. It is not literally a piece of shit. No, you're
thinking of a different sect.

THE LOST AND FOUND

The lost and found is not a sad place for things. At the lost and found, all things are equal. A diamond brooch and a whoopee cushion are just two lost things at the lost and found. That is not a sad thing. It would be sad if they were people, not things. It would be sad if the two lost things were not a diamond brooch and a whoopee cushion but you and me. It would be sad because we'd know we were lost, hoping to be found, and not quite believing we ever will. But things can't hope. And perhaps they can't truly be lost either.

No Ideas but in Things

A thing had an idea. Another thing had a different idea.

"Listen to my idea," said the first thing.

"Shoot," said the second.

"Well," said the first thing, "I was thinking, and thinking gave me ideas."

"Yes?"

"And one of my ideas was, oh, I don't know how to put it, oh, all right, one of my ideas was kind of—different."

"You stole my idea!" the second thing said. "You bastard! You fucking bastard! You stole my idea!"

SIMULACRA

It wasn't the thing itself, but rather a simulacrum. An analog, a representation, but not the real deal, and it had no business passing itself off as such—that's what I call false pretenses.

Authenticity—nobody cares a whit about authenticity anymore. It's a crying shame.

Take this text, for instance. It purports to be a simulacrum, a text about a simulacrum, yet just what it's a simulacrum of, we're not told. So is this a text or a simulacrum of a text? Is it perhaps a template, a blueprint for a text, or numerous, even infinite texts?

It wasn't a plum, but rather a simulacrum of a plum. It wasn't an orgasm, but rather a simulacrum of an orgasm. It wasn't a cold day in May, but rather a simulacrum of a cold day in May. It was an analog of whatever you love the most, a representation of peace on earth.

And that would just have to do.

CHICKEN GOODBYE

The last time she cooked for him, he said, "This is very good. What do you call it?"

"Chicken Goodbye," she replied.

ABOUT THE AUTHOR

Called "one of the innovators of the short short story" by *Publishers Weekly*, Peter Cherches has published seven volumes of fiction and nonfiction since 2013. His writing has also appeared in scores of magazines, anthologies and websites, including *Harper's*, *Bomb*, *Semiotext(e)*, and *Fiction International*, as well as Billy Collins' *Poetry 180*. A native of Brooklyn, New York, he is also a jazz singer and lyricist.

ALSO FROM BAMBOO DART PRESS

by Peter Cherches

Tracks: Memoirs from a Life with Music (2021)

In these mini memoirs, Peter Cherches revisits musical experiences, pleasures, and obsessions that have punctuated his life. A singer and lyricist as well as "one of the innovators of the short short story" (*Publishers Weekly*), Cherches writes here from the perspective of a voracious listener for whom music is a constant companion. Whether reminiscing about the joys of musical discovery or paying tribute to musicians who have inspired him, Cherches shares his passions with verve and wit. From an early baptism in Beatlemania, to adolescent encounters with free jazz, to expeditions for local musical treasures around the world, this collection of singles in prose is a testament to the sustaining power of music in our lives.

Masks: Stories from a Pandemic (2022)

In the spring of 2020, shortly after he had started wearing a face mask outside his home, Peter Cherches began writing about masks, literally the face of COVID-19. These 16 stories, written between April and December of that year, capture the surreal experience of living through a global pandemic and all its attendant challenges—personal, political, and social. This small volume is both a mask-muffled cry and a full-throated belly laugh. Reactions are to be expected, and are no cause for concern.

BAMBOO
DART
PRESS

112 N. Harvard Ave. #65
Claremont, CA 91711

chapbooks@bamboodartpress.com

www.bamboodartpress.com